Defoe
Abbott
Marx
Hardy
Melville
Montaigne
Machiavelli
Chesterton
Cooper
Emerson
Haggard
Joyce
Austen
Hugo
Eliot
Grimm
Carroll
Christie
Stoker
Wilde
Maupassant
Byron
Molière
Schiller
Garnett
Goethe
Einstein
Fitzgerald
Engels
Hawthorne
Smith
Kafka
Hall
Cotton
Kipling
Doyle
Dostoyevsky
Baum
Henry
Nietzsche
Leslie
Dumas
Flaubert
Turgenev
Balzac
Stockton
Vatsyayana
Crane
Burroughs
Verne
Curtis
Tocqueville
Whitman
Gogol
Vinci
Homer
Widger
Tolstoy
Busch
Darwin
Thoreau
Potter
Freud
Zola
Twain
Scott
Plato
Kant
Jowett
Stevenson
Lawrence
Dickens
Harte
Hesse
Andersen
Burton
London
Descartes
Cervantes
Poe
Aristotle
Wells
Voltaire
Cooke
Hale
James
Hastings
Bunner
Shakespeare
Irving
Richter
Chambers
da
Shaw
Benedict
Alcott
Doré
Swift
Dante
Chekhov
Wodehouse
Pushkin
Newton

AF303442

 tredition®

tredition was established in 2006 by Sandra Latusseck and Soenke Schulz. Based in Hamburg, Germany, tredition offers publishing solutions to authors and publishing houses, combined with world-wide distribution of printed and digital book content. tredition is uniquely positioned to enable authors and publishing houses to create books on their own terms and without conventional manu-facturing risks.

For more information please visit: www.tredition.com

TREDITION CLASSICS

This book is part of the TREDITION CLASSICS series. The creators of this series are united by passion for literature and driven by the intention of making all public domain books available in printed format again - worldwide. Most TREDITION CLASSICS titles have been out of print and off the bookstore shelves for decades. At tredi-tion we believe that a great book never goes out of style and that its value is eternal. Several mostly non-profit literature projects provide content to tredition. To support their good work, tredition donates a portion of the proceeds from each sold copy. As a reader of a TREDITION CLASSICS book, you support our mission to save many of the amazing works of world literature from oblivion. See all available books at www.tredition.com.

Project Gutenberg

The content for this book has been graciously provided by Project Gutenberg. Project Gutenberg is a non-profit organization founded by Michael Hart in 1971 at the University of Illinois. The mission of Project Gutenberg is simple: To encourage the creation and distribu-tion of eBooks. Project Gutenberg is the first and largest collection of public domain eBooks.

Harold : the Last of the Saxon Kings

Volume 10

Baron Edward Bulwer Lytton Lytton

Imprint

This book is part of TREDITION CLASSICS

Author: Baron Edward Bulwer Lytton Lytton
Cover design: Buchgut, Berlin – Germany

Publisher: tredition GmbH, Hamburg - Germany
ISBN: 978-3-8424-3113-3

www.tredition.com
www.tredition.de

Copyright:
The content of this book is sourced from the public domain.

The intention of the TREDITION CLASSICS series is to make world literature in the public domain available in printed format. Literary enthusiasts and organizations, such as Project Gutenberg, world-wide have scanned and digitally edited the original texts. tredition has subsequently formatted and redesigned the content into a modern reading layout. Therefore, we cannot guarantee the exact reproduction of the original format of a particular historic edition. Please also note that no modifications have been made to the spelling, therefore it may differ from the orthography used today.

BOOK X.

THE SACRIFICE ON THE ALTAR.

CHAPTER I.

The good Bishop Alred, now raised to the See of York, had been summoned from his cathedral seat by Edward, who had indeed undergone a severe illness, during the absence of Harold; and that illness had been both preceded and followed by mystical presentiments of the evil days that were to fall on England after his death. He had therefore sent for the best and the holiest prelate in his realm, to advise and counsel with.

The bishop had returned to his lodging in London (which was in a Benedictine Abbey, not far from the Aldgate) late one evening, from visiting the King at his rural palace of Havering; and he was seated alone in his cell, musing over an interview with Edward, which had evidently much disturbed him, when the door was abruptly thrown open, and pushing aside in haste the monk, who was about formally to announce him, a man so travel-stained in garb, and of a mien so disordered, rushed in, that Alred gazed at first as on a stranger, and not till the intruder spoke did he recognise Harold the Earl. Even then, so wild was the Earl's eye, so dark his brow, and so livid his cheek, that it rather seemed the ghost of the man than the man himself. Closing the door on the monk, the Earl stood a moment on the threshold, with a breast heaving with emotions which he sought in vain to master; and, as if resigning the effort, he sprang forward, clasped the prelate's knees, bowed his head on his lap, and sobbed aloud. The good bishop, who had known all the sons of Godwin from their infancy, and to whom Harold was as dear as his own child, folding his hands over the Earl's head, soothingly murmured a benediction.

"No, no," cried the Earl, starting to his feet, and tossing the dishevelled hair from his eyes, "bless me not yet! Hear my tale first, and then say what comfort, what refuge, thy Church can bestow!"

Hurriedly then the Earl poured forth the dark story, already known to the reader, — the prison at Belrem, the detention at William's court, the fears, the snares, the discourse by the riverside, the oath over the relics. This told, he continued, "I found myself in the open air, and knew not, till the light of the sun smote me, what might have passed into my soul. I was, before, as a corpse which a witch raises from the dead, endows with a spirit not its own — passive to her hand — life-like, not living. Then, then it was as if a demon had passed from my body, laughing scorn at the foul things it had made the clay do. O, father, father! is there not absolution from this oath, — an oath I dare not keep? rather perjure myself than betray my land!"

The prelate's face was as pale as Harold's, and it was some moments before he could reply.

"The Church can loose and unloose — such is its delegated authority. But speak on; what saidst thou at the last to William?"

"I know not, remember not — aught save these words. 'Now, then, give me those for whom I placed myself in thy power; let me restore Haco to his fatherland, and Wolnoth to his mother's kiss, and wend home my way.' And, saints in heaven! what was the answer of this caitiff Norman, with his glittering eye and venomed smile? 'Haco thou shalt have, for he is an orphan and an uncle's love is not so hot as to burn from a distance; but Wolnoth, thy mother's son, must stay with me as a hostage for thine own faith. Godwin's hostages are released; Harold's hostage I retain: it is but a form, yet these forms are the bonds of princes.'

"I looked at him, and his eye quailed. And I said, 'That is not in the compact.' And William answered, 'No, but it is the seal to it.'

Then I turned from the Duke and I called my brother to my side, and I said, 'Over the seas have I come for thee. Mount thy steed and ride by my side, for I will not leave the land without thee.' And Wolnoth answered, 'Nay, Duke William tells me that he hath made treaties with thee, for which I am still to be the hostage; and Normandy has grown my home, and I love William as my lord.' Hot words followed, and Wolnoth, chafed, refused entreaty and command, and suffered me to see that his heart was not with England! O, mother, mother, how shall I meet thine eye! So I returned with Haco. The moment I set foot on my native England, that moment her form seemed to rise from the tall cliffs, her voice to speak in the winds! All the glamour by which I had been bound, forsook me; and I sprang forward in scorn, above the fear of the dead men's bones. Miserable overcraft of the snarer! Had my simple word alone bound me, or that word been ratified after slow and deliberate thought, by the ordinary oaths that appeal to God, far stronger the bond upon my soul than the mean surprise, the covert tricks, the insult and the mocking fraud. But as I rode on, the oath pursued me—pale spectres mounted behind me on my steed, ghastly fingers pointed from the welkin; and then suddenly, O my father—I who, sincere in my simple faith, had, as thou knowest too well, never bowed submissive conscience to priest and Church—then suddenly I felt the might of some power, surer guide than that haughty conscience which had so in the hour of need betrayed me! Then I recognised that supreme tribunal, that mediator between Heaven and man, to which I might come with the dire secret of my soul, and say, as I say now, on my bended knee, O father—father—bid me die, or absolve me from my oath!"

Then Alred rose erect, and replied, "Did I need subterfuge, O son, I would say, that William himself hath released thy bond, in detaining the hostage against the spirit of the guilty compact; that in the very words themselves of the oath, lies the release—'if God aid thee.' God aids no child to parricide—and thou art England's child! But all school casuistry is here a meanness. Plain is the law, that oaths extorted by compulsion, through fraud and in fear, the Church hath the right to loose: plainer still the law of God and of man, that an oath to commit crime it is a deadlier sin to keep than to forfeit. Wherefore, not absolving thee from the misdeed of a vow that, if trusting more to God's providence and less to man's vain strength and dim wit, thou wouldst never have uttered even for England's sake— leaving her to the angels;—not, I say, absolving thee from that sin, but pausing yet to decide what penance and atonement to fix to its committal, I do in the name of the Power whose priest I am, forbid thee to fulfil the oath; I do release and absolve thee from all obligation thereto. And if in this I exceed my authority as Romish priest, I do but accomplish my duties as living man. To these grey hairs I take the sponsorship. Before this holy cross, kneel, O my son, with me, and pray that a life of truth and virtue may atone the madness of an hour."

So by the crucifix knelt the warrior and the priest.

CHAPTER II.

All other thought had given way to Harold's impetuous yearning to throw himself upon the Church, to hear his doom from the purest and wisest of its Saxon preachers. Had the prelate deemed his vow irrefragable, he would have died the Roman's death, rather than live the traitor's life; and strange indeed was the revolution created in this man's character, that he, "so self-dependent," he who had hitherto deemed himself his sole judge below of cause and action, now felt the whole life of his life committed to the word of a cloistered shaveling. All other thought had given way to that fiery impulse— home, mother, Edith, king, power, policy, ambition! Till the weight was from his soul, he was as an outlaw in his native land. But when the next sun rose, and that awful burthen was lifted from his heart and his being—when his own calm sense, returning, sanctioned the fiat of the priest,—when, though with deep shame and rankling remorse at the memory of the vow, he yet felt exonerated, not from the guilt of having made, but the deadlier guilt of fulfilling it—all the objects of existence resumed their natural interest, softened and chastened, but still vivid in the heart restored to humanity. But from that time, Harold's stern philosophy and stoic ethics were shaken to the dust; re-created, as it were, by the breath of religion, he adopted its tenets even after the fashion of his age. The secret of his shame, the error of his conscience, humbled him. Those unlettered monks whom he had so despised, how had he lost the right to stand aloof from their control! how had his wisdom, and his strength, and his courage, met unguarded the hour of temptation!

Yes, might the time come, when England could spare him from her side! when he, like Sweyn the outlaw, could pass a pilgrim to the Holy Sepulchre, and there, as the creed of the age taught, win full pardon for the single lie of his truthful life, and regain the old peace of his stainless conscience!

There are sometimes event and season in the life of man the hardest and most rational, when he is driven perforce to faith the most implicit and submissive; as the storm drives the wings of the petrel over a measureless sea, till it falls tame, and rejoicing at refuge, on the sails of some lonely ship. Seasons when difficulties, against which reason seems stricken into palsy, leave him bewildered in dismay —when darkness, which experience cannot pierce, wraps the conscience, as sudden night wraps the traveller in the desert— when error entangles his feet in its inextricable web—when, still desirous of the right, he sees before him but a choice of evil; and the Angel of the Past, with a flaming sword, closes on him the gates of the Future. Then, Faith flashes on him, with a light from the cloud. Then, he clings to Prayer as a drowning wretch to the plank. Then, that solemn authority which clothes the Priest, as the interpreter between the soul and the Divinity, seizes on the heart that trembles with terror and joy; then, that mysterious recognition of Atonement, of sacrifice, of purifying lustration (mystery which lies hid in the core of all religions), smoothes the frown on the Past, removes the flaming sword from the future. The Orestes escapes from the hounding Furies, and follows the oracle to the spot where the cleansing dews shall descend on the expiated guilt.

He who hath never known in himself, nor marked in another, such strange crisis in human fate, cannot judge of the strength and the weakness it bestows. But till he can so judge, the spiritual part of all history is to him a blank scroll, a sealed volume. He cannot comprehend what drove the fierce Heathen, cowering and humbled, into the fold of the Church; what peopled Egypt with eremites; what lined the roads of Europe and Asia with pilgrim homicides; what, in the elder world, while Jove yet reigned on Olympus, is couched in the dim traditions of the expiation of Apollo, the joy-god, descending into Hades; or why the sinner went blithe and light-hearted from the healing lustrations of Eleusis. In all these solemn riddles of the Jove world and the Christ's is involved the imperious necessity that man hath of repentance and atonement: through their clouds, as a rainbow, shines the covenant that reconciles the God and the man.

Now Life with strong arms plucked the reviving Harold to itself. Already the news of his return had spread through the city, and his chamber soon swarmed with joyous welcomes and anxious friends. But the first congratulations over, each had tidings that claimed his instant attention, to relate. His absence had sufficed to loosen half the links of that ill-woven empire.

All the North was in arms. Northumbria had revolted as one man, from the tyrannous cruelty of Tostig; the insurgents had marched upon York; Tostig had fled in dismay, none as yet knew whither. The sons of Algar had sallied forth from their Mercian fortresses, and were now in the ranks of the Northumbrians, who it was rumoured had selected Morcar (the elder) in the place of Tostig.

Amidst these disasters, the King's health was fast decaying; his mind seemed bewildered and distraught; dark ravings of evil portent that had escaped from his lip in his mystic reveries and visions, had spread abroad, bandied with all natural exaggerations, from lip to lip. The country was in one state of gloomy and vague apprehension.

But all would go well, now Harold the great Earl—Harold the stout, and the wise, and the loved—had come back to his native land!

In feeling himself thus necessary to England,—all eyes, all hopes, all hearts turned to him, and to him alone,—Harold shook the evil memories from his soul, as a lion shakes the dews from his mane. His intellect, that seemed to have burned dim and through smoke in scenes unfamiliar to its exercise, rose at once equal to the occasion. His words reassured the most despondent. His orders were prompt and decisive. While, to and fro, went forth his bodes and his riders, he himself leaped on his horse, and rode fast to Havering.

At length that sweet and lovely retreat broke on his sight, as a bower through the bloom of a garden. This was Edward's favourite abode: he had built it himself for his private devotions, allured by its woody solitudes and gloom of its copious verdure. Here it was said, that once that night, wandering through the silent glades, and musing on heaven, the loud song of the nightingales had disturbed his devotions; with vexed and impatient soul, he had prayed that the music might be stilled: and since then, never more the nightingale was heard in the shades of Havering! Threading the woodland, melancholy yet glorious with the hues of autumn, Harold reached the low and humble gate of the timber edifice, all covered with creepers and young ivy; and in a few moments more he stood in the presence of the King.

Edward raised himself with pain from the couch on which he was reclined [204], beneath a canopy supported by columns and surmounted by carved symbols of the bell towers of Jerusalem: and his languid face brightened at the sight of Harold. Behind the King stood a man with a Danish battle-axe in his hand, the captain of the royal house- carles, who, on a sign from the King, withdrew.

"Thou art come back, Harold," said Edward then, in a feeble voice; and the Earl drawing near, was grieved and shocked at the alteration of his face. "Thou art come back, to aid this benumbed hand, from which the earthly sceptre is about to fall. Hush! for it is so, and I rejoice." Then examining Harold's features, yet pale with recent emotions, and now saddened by sympathy with the King, he resumed: "Well, man of this world, that went forth confiding in thine own strength, and in the faith of men of the world like thee,— well, were my warnings prophetic, or art thou contented with thy mission?"

"Alas!" said Harold, mournfully. "Thy wisdom was greater than mine, O King; and dread the snares laid for me and our native land, under pretext of a promise made by thee to Count William, that he should reign in England, should he be your survivor."

Edward's face grew troubled and embarrassed. "Such promise," he said, falteringly, "when I knew not the laws of England, nor that a realm could not pass like house and hyde by a man's single testament, might well escape from my thoughts, never too bent upon earthly affairs. But I marvel not that my cousin's mind is more tenacious and mundane. And verily, in those vague words, and from thy visit, I see the Future dark with fate and crimson with blood."

Then Edward's eyes grew locked and set, staring into space; and even that reverie, though it awed him, relieved Harold of much disquietude, for he rightly conjectured, that on waking from it Edward would press him no more as to those details, and dilemmas of conscience, of which he felt that the arch-worshipper of relics was no fitting judge.

When the King, with a heavy sigh, evinced return from the world of vision, he stretched forth to Harold his wan, transparent hand, and said:

"Thou seest the ring on this finger; it comes to me from above, a merciful token to prepare my soul for death. Perchance thou mayest have heard that once an aged pilgrim stopped me on my way from God's House, and asked for alms—and I, having nought else on my person to bestow, drew from my finger a ring, and gave it to him, and the old man went his way, blessing me."

"I mind me well of thy gentle charity," said the Earl; "for the pilgrim bruited it abroad as he passed, and much talk was there of it."

The King smiled faintly. "Now this was years ago. It so chanced this year, that certain Englishers, on their way from the Holy Land, fell in with two pilgrims—and these last questioned them much of me. And one, with face venerable and benign, drew forth a ring and said, 'When thou reachest England, give thou this to the King's own hand, and say, by this token, that on Twelfth-Day Eve he shall be with me. For what he gave to me, will I prepare recompense without bound; and already the saints deck for the new comer the halls where the worm never gnaws and the moth never frets.' 'And who,' asked my subjects amazed, 'who shall we say, speaketh thus to us?' And the pilgrim answered, 'He on whose breast leaned the Son of God, and my name is John!' [205] Wherewith the apparition vanished. This is the ring I gave to the pilgrim; on the fourteenth night from thy parting, miraculously returned to me. Wherefore, Harold, my time here is brief, and I rejoice that thy coming delivers me up from the cares of state to the preparation of my soul for the joyous day."

Harold, suspecting under this incredible mission some wily device of the Norman, who, by thus warning Edward (of whose precarious health he was well aware), might induce his timorous conscience to take steps for the completion of the old promise,—Harold, we say, thus suspecting, in vain endeavoured to combat the King's presentiments, but Edward interrupted him, with displeased firmness of look and tone:

"Come not thou, with thy human reasonings, between my soul and the messenger divine; but rather nerve and prepare thyself for the dire calamities that lie greeding in the days to come! Be thine, things temporal. All the land is in rebellion. Anlaf, whom thy coming dismissed, hath just wearied me with sad tales of bloodshed and ravage. Go and hear him;—go hear the bodes of thy brother Tostig, who wait without in our hall;—go, take axe, and take shield, and the men of earth's war, and do justice and right; and on thy return thou shalt see with what rapture sublime a Christian King can soar aloft from his throne! Go!"

More moved, and more softened, than in the former day he had been with Edward's sincere, if fanatical piety, Harold, turning aside to conceal his face, said:

"Would, O royal Edward, that my heart, amidst worldly cares, were as pure and serene as thine! But, at least, what erring mortal may do to guard this realm, and face the evils thou foreseest in the Far—that will I do; and perchance, then, in my dying hour, God's pardon and peace may descend on me!" He spoke, and went.

The accounts he received from Anlaf (a veteran Anglo-Dane), were indeed more alarming than he had yet heard. Morcar, the bold son of Algar, was already proclaimed, by the rebels, Earl of Northumbria; the shires of Nottingham, Derby, and Lincoln, had poured forth their hardy Dane populations on his behalf. All Mercia was in arms under his brother Edwin; and many of the Cymrian chiefs had already joined the ally of the butchered Gryffyth.

Not a moment did the Earl lose in proclaiming the Herr-bann; sheaves of arrows were splintered, and the fragments, as announcing the War- Fyrd, were sent from thegn to thegn, and town to town. Fresh messengers were despatched to Gurth to collect the whole force of his own earldom, and haste by quick marches to London; and, these preparations made, Harold returned to the metropolis, and with a heavy heart sought his mother, as his next care.

Githa was already prepared for his news; for Haco had of his own accord gone to break the first shock of disappointment. There was in this youth a noiseless sagacity that seemed ever provident for Harold. With his sombre, smileless cheek, and gloom of beauty, bowed as if beneath the weight of some invisible doom, he had already become linked indissolubly with the Earl's fate, as its angel,—but as its angel of darkness!

To Harold's intense relief, Githa stretched forth her hands as he entered, and said, "Thou hast failed me, but against thy will! grieve not; I am content!"

"Now our Lady be blessed, mother—"

"I have told her," said Haco, who was standing, with arms folded, by the fire, the blaze of which reddened fitfully his hueless countenance with its raven hair; "I have told thy mother that Wolnoth loves his captivity, and enjoys the cage. And the lady hath had comfort in my words."

"Not in thine only, son of Sweyn, but in those of fate; for before thy coming I prayed against the long blind yearning of my heart, prayed that Wolnoth might not cross the sea with his kinsmen."

"How!" exclaimed the Earl, astonished.

Githa took his arm, and led him to the farther end of the ample chamber, as if out of the hearing of Haco, who turned his face towards the fire, and gazed into the fierce blaze with musing, unwinking eyes.

"Couldst thou think, Harold, that in thy journey, that on the errand of so great fear and hope, I could sit brooding in my chair, and count the stitches on the tremulous hangings? No; day by day have I sought the lore of Hilda, and at night I have watched with her by the fount, and the elm, and the tomb; and I know that thou hast gone through dire peril; the prison, the war, and the snare; and I know also, that his Fylgia hath saved the life of my Wolnoth; for had he returned to his native land, he had returned but to a bloody grave!"

"Says Hilda this?" said the Earl, thoughtfully.

"So say the Vala, the rune, and the Scin-laeca! and such is the doom that now darkens the brow of Haco! Seest thou not that the hand of death is in the hush of the smileless lip, and the glance of the unjoyous eye?"

"Nay, it is but the thought born to captive youth, and nurtured in solitary dreams. Thou hast seen Hilda?—and Edith, my mother? Edith is—"

"Well," said Githa, kindly, for she sympathised with that love which Godwin would have condemned, "though she grieved deeply after thy departure, and would sit for hours gazing into space, and moaning. But even ere Hilda divined thy safe return, Edith knew it; I was beside her at the time; she started up, and cried, 'Harold is in England!'—'How?—Why thinkest thou so?' said I. And Edith answered, 'I feel it by the touch of the earth, by the breath of the air.' This is more than love, Harold. I knew two twins who had the same instinct of each other's comings and goings, and were present each to each even when absent: Edith is twin to my soul. Thou goest to her now, Harold: thou wilt find there thy sister Thyra. The child hath drooped of late, and I besought Hilda to revive her, with herb and charm. Thou wilt come back, ere thou departest to aid Tostig, thy brother, and tell me how Hilda hath prospered with my ailing child?"

"I will, my mother. Be cheered!—Hilda is a skilful nurse. And now bless thee, that thou hast not reproached me that my mission failed to fulfil my promise. Welcome even our kinswoman's sayings, sith they comfort thee for the loss of thy darling!"

Then Harold left the room, mounted his steed, and rode through the town towards the bridge. He was compelled to ride slowly through the streets, for he was recognised; and cheapman and mechanic rushed from house and from stall to hail the Man of the Land and the Time.

"All is safe now in England, for Harold is come back!" They seemed joyous as the children of the mariner, when, with wet garments, he struggles to shore through the storm. And kind and loving were Harold's looks and brief words, as he rode with vailed bonnet through the swarming streets.

At length he cleared the town and the bridge; and the yellowing boughs of the orchards drooped over the road towards the Roman home, when, as he spurred his steed, he heard behind him hoofs as in pursuit, looked back, and beheld Haco. He drew rein,—"What wantest thou, my nephew?"

"Thee!" answered Haco, briefly, as he gained his side. "Thy companionship."

"Thanks, Haco; but I pray thee to stay in my mother's house, for I would fain ride alone."

"Spurn me not from thee, Harold! This England is to me the land of the stranger; in thy mother's house I feel but the more the orphan. Henceforth I have devoted to thee my life! And my life my dead and dread father hath left to thee, as a doom or a blessing; wherefore cleave I to thy side;—cleave we in life and in death to each other!"

An undefined and cheerless thrill shot through the Earl's heart as the youth spoke thus; and the remembrance that Haco's counsel had first induced him to abandon his natural hardy and gallant manhood, meet wile by wile, and thus suddenly entangle him in his own meshes, had already mingled an inexpressible bitterness with his pity and affection for his brother's son. But, struggling against that uneasy sentiment, as unjust towards one to whose counsel— however sinister, and now repented—he probably owed, at least, his safety and deliverance, he replied gently:

"I accept thy trust and thy love, Haco! Ride with me, then; but pardon a dull comrade, for when the soul communes with itself the lip is silent."

"True," said Haco, "and I am no babbler. Three things are ever silent: Thought, Destiny, and the Grave."

Each then, pursuing his own fancies, rode on fast, and side by side; the long shadows of declining day struggling with a sky of unusual brightness, and thrown from the dim forest trees and the distant hillocks. Alternately through shade and through light rode they on; the bulls gazing on them from holt and glade, and the boom of the bittern sounding in its peculiar mournfulness of toile as it rose from the dank pools that glistened in the western sun.

It was always by the rear of the house, where stood the ruined temple, so associated with the romance of his life, that Harold approached the home of the Vala; and as now the hillock, with its melancholy diadem of stones, came in view, Haco for the first time broke the silence.

"Again—as in a dream!" he said, abruptly. "Hill, ruin, grave-mound— but where the tall image of the mighty one?"

"Hast thou then seen this spot before?" asked the Earl.

"Yea, as an infant here was I led by my father Sweyn; here too, from thy house yonder, dim seen through the fading leaves, on the eve before I left this land for the Norman, here did I wander alone; and there, by that altar, did the great Vala of the North chaunt her runes for my future."

"Alas! thou too!" murmured Harold; and then he asked aloud, "What said she?"

"That thy life and mine crossed each other in the skein; that I should save thee from a great peril, and share with thee a greater."

"Ah, youth," answered Harold, bitterly, "these vain prophecies of human wit guard the soul from no anger. They mislead us by riddles which our hot hearts interpret according to their own desires. Keep thou fast to youth's simple wisdom, and trust only to the pure spirit and the watchful God."

He suppressed a groan as he spoke, and springing from his steed, which he left loose, advanced up the hill. When he had gained the height, he halted, and made sign to Haco, who had also dismounted, to do the same. Half way down the side of the slope which faced the ruined peristyle, Haco beheld a maiden, still young, and of beauty surpassing all that the court of Normandy boasted of female loveliness. She was seated on the sward;—while a girl younger, and scarcely indeed grown into womanhood, reclined at her feet, and leaning her cheek upon her hand, seemed hushed in listening attention. In the face of the younger girl Haco recognised Thyra, the last-born of Githa, though he had but once seen her before—the day ere he left England for the Norman court—for the face of the girl was but little changed, save that the eye was more mournful, and the cheek was paler.

And Harold's betrothed was singing, in the still autumn air, to Harold's sister. The song chosen was on that subject the most popular with the Saxon poets, the mystic life, death, and resurrection of the fabled Phoenix, and this rhymeless song, in its old native flow, may yet find some grace in the modern ear.

THE LAY OF THE PHOENIX. [206]

"Shineth far hence—so
  Sing the wise elders
Far to the fire-east
  The fairest of lands.

Daintily dight is that
  Dearest of joy fields;
Breezes all balmy-filled
  Glide through its groves.

There to the blest, ope
  The high doors of heaven,
Sweetly sweep earthward
  Their wavelets of song.

Frost robes the sward not,
  Rusheth no hail-steel;
Wind-cloud ne'er wanders,
  Ne'er falleth the rain.

Warding the woodholt,
  Girt with gay wonder,
Sheen with the plumy shine,
  Phoenix abides.

Lord of the Lleod, [207]
  Whose home is the air,
Winters a thousand
  Abideth the bird.

Hapless and heavy then
  Waxeth the hazy wing;
Year-worn and old in the
  Whirl of the earth.

Then the high holt-top,
  Mounting, the bird soars;
There, where the winds sleep,
  He buildeth a nest;—

Gums the most precious, and
  Balms of the sweetest,
Spices and odours, he
  Weaves in the nest.

There, in that sun-ark, lo,
  Waiteth he wistful;
Summer comes smiling, lo,
  Rays smite the pile!

Burden'd with eld-years, and
  Weary with slow time,
Slow in his odour-nest
  Burneth the bird.

Up from those ashes, then,
  Springeth a rare fruit;
Deep in the rare fruit
  There coileth a worm.

Weaving bliss-meshes
  Around and around it,
Silent and blissful, the
  Worm worketh on.

Lo, from the airy web,
  Blooming and brightsome,
Young and exulting, the
  Phoenix breaks forth.

Round him the birds troop,
  Singing and hailing;
Wings of all glories
  Engarland the king.

Hymning and hailing,
  Through forest and sun-air,
Hymning and hailing,
  And speaking him 'King.'

High flies the phoenix,
  Escaped from the worm-web
He soars in the sunlight,
  He bathes in the dew.

He visits his old haunts,
  The holt and the sun-hill;
The founts of his youth, and
  The fields of his love.

The stars in the welkin,
  The blooms on the earth,
Are glad in his gladness,
  Are young in his youth.

While round him the birds troop,
  the Hosts of the Himmel, [208]
Blisses of music, and
  Glories of wings;

Hymning and hailing,
  And filling the sun-air
With music, and glory
  And praise of the King."

As the lay ceased, Thyra said:

"Ah, Edith, who would not brave the funeral pyre to live again like the phoenix!"

"Sweet sister mine," answered Edith, "the singer doth mean to image out in the phoenix the rising of our Lord, in whom we all live again."

And Thyra said, mournfully:

"But the phoenix sees once more the haunts of his youth—the things and places dear to him in his life before. Shall we do the same, O Edith?"

"It is the persons we love that make beautiful the haunts we have known," answered the betrothed. "Those persons at least we shall behold again, and whenever they are—there is heaven."

Harold could restrain himself no longer. With one bound he was at Edith's side, and with one wild cry of joy he clasped her to his heart.

"I knew that thou wouldst come to-night—I knew it, Harold," murmured the betrothed.

CHAPTER III.

While, full of themselves, Harold and Edith wandered, hand in hand, through the neighbouring glades—while into that breast which had forestalled, at least, in this pure and sublime union, the wife's privilege to soothe and console, the troubled man poured out the tale of the sole trial from which he had passed with defeat and shame,— Haco drew near to Thyra, and sate down by her side. Each was strangely attracted towards the other; there was something congenial in the gloom which they shared in common; though in the girl the sadness was soft and resigned, in the youth it was stern and solemn. They conversed in whispers, and their talk was strange for companions so young; for, whether suggested by Edith's song, or the neighbourhood of the Saxon grave-stone, which gleamed on their eyes, grey and wan through the crommell, the theme they selected was of death. As if fascinated, as children often are, by the terrors of the Dark King, they dwelt on those images with which the northern fancy has associated the eternal rest, on—the shroud and the worm, and the mouldering bones—on the gibbering ghost, and the sorcerer's spell that could call the spectre from the grave. They talked of the pain of the parting soul, parting while earth was yet fair, youth fresh, and joy not yet ripened from the blossom—of the wistful lingering look which glazing eyes would give to the latest sunlight it should behold on earth; and then he pictured the shivering and naked soul, forced from the reluctant clay, wandering through cheerless space to the intermediate tortures, which the Church taught that none were so pure as not for a whole to undergo; and hearing, as it wandered, the knell of the muffled bells and the burst of unavailing prayer. At length Haco paused abruptly and said:

"But thou, cousin, hast before thee love and sweet life, and these discourses are not for thee."

Thyra shook her head mournfully:

"Not so, Haco; for when Hilda consulted the runes, while, last night, she mingled the herbs for my pain, which rests ever hot and sharp here," and the girl laid her hand on her breast, "I saw that her face grew dark and overcast; and I felt, as I looked, that my doom was set. And when thou didst come so noiselessly to my side, with thy sad, cold eyes, O Haco, methought I saw the Messenger of Death. But thou art strong, Haco, and life will be long for thee; let us talk of life."

Haco stooped down and pressed his lips upon the girl's pale forehead.

"Kiss me too, Thyra."

The child kissed him, and they sate silent and close by each other, while the sun set.

And as the stars rose, Harold and Edith joined them. Harold's face was serene in the starlight, for the pure soul of his betrothed had breathed peace into his own; and, in his willing superstition, he felt as if, now restored to his guardian angel, the dead men's bones had released their unhallowed hold.

But suddenly Edith's hand trembled in his, and her form shuddered. —
Her eyes were fixed upon those of Haco.

"Forgive me, young kinsman, that I forget thee so long," said the Earl. "This is my brother's son, Edith; thou hast not, that I remember, seen him before?"

"Yes, yes;" said Edith, falteringly.

"When, and where?"

Edith's soul answered the question, "In a dream;" but her lips were silent.

And Haco, rising, took her by the hand, while the Earl turned to his sister—that sister whom he was pledged to send to the Norman court; and Thyra said, plaintively:

"Take me in thine arms, Harold, and wrap thy mantle round me, for the air is cold."

The Earl lifted the child to his breast, and gazed on her cheek long and wistfully; then questioning her tenderly, he took her within the house; and Edith followed with Haco.

"Is Hilda within?" asked the son of Sweyn.

"Nay, she hath been in the forest since noon," answered Edith with an effort, for she could not recover her awe of his presence.

"Then," said Haco, halting at the threshold, "I will go across the woodland to your house, Harold, and prepare your ceorls for your coming."

"I shall tarry here till Hilda returns," answered Harold, and it may be late in the night ere I reach home; but Sexwolf already hath my orders. At sunrise we return to London, and thence we march on the insurgents."

"All shall be ready. Farewell, noble Edith; and thou, Thyra my cousin, one kiss more to our meeting again." The child fondly held out her arms to him, and as she kissed his cheek whispered:

"In the grave, Haco!"

The young man drew his mantle around him, and moved away. But he did not mount his steed, which still grazed by the road; while Harold's, more familiar with the place, had found its way to the stall; nor did he take his path through the glades to the house of his kinsman. Entering the Druid temple, he stood musing by the Teuton tomb. The night grew deeper and deeper, the stars more luminous and the air more hushed, when a voice close at his side, said, clear and abrupt:

"What does Youth the restless, by Death the still?"

It was the peculiarity of Haco, that nothing ever seemed to startle or surprise him. In that brooding boyhood, the solemn, quiet, and sad experience all fore-armed, of age, had something in it terrible and preternatural; so without lifting his eyes from the stone, he answered:

"How sayest thou, O Hilda, that the dead are still?" Hilda placed her hand on his shoulder, and stooped to look into his face.

"Thy rebuke is just, son of Sweyn. In Time, and in the Universe, there is no stillness! Through all eternity the state impossible to the soul is repose!—So again thou art in thy native land?"

"And for what end, Prophetess? I remember, when but an infant, who till then had enjoyed the common air and the daily sun, thou didst rob me evermore of childhood and youth. For thou didst say to my father, that 'dark was the woof of my fate, and that its most glorious hour should be its last!'"

"But thou wert surely too childlike, (see thee now as thou wert then, stretched on the grass, and playing with thy father's falcon!) — too childlike to heed my words."

"Does the new ground reject the germs of the sower, or the young heart the first lessons of wonder and awe? Since then, Prophetess, Night hath been my comrade, and Death my familiar. Rememberest thou again the hour when, stealing, a boy, from Harold's house in his absence — the night ere I left my land — I stood on this mound by thy side? Then did I tell thee that the sole soft thought that relieved the bitterness of my soul, when all the rest of my kinsfolk seemed to behold in me but the heir of Sweyn, the outlaw and homicide, was the love that I bore to Harold; but that that love itself was mournful and bodeful as the hwata [209] of distant sorrow. And thou didst take me, O Prophetess, to thy bosom, and thy cold kiss touched my lips and my brow; and there, beside this altar and grave-mound, by leaf and by water, by staff and by song, thou didst bid me take comfort; for that as the mouse gnawed the toils of the lion, so the exile obscure should deliver from peril the pride and the prince of my House — that, from that hour with the skein of his fate should mine be entwined; and his fate was that of kings and of kingdoms. And then, when the joy flushed my cheek, and methought youth came back in warmth to the night of my soul — then, Hilda, I asked thee if my life would be spared till I had redeemed the name of my father. Thy seidstaff passed over the leaves that, burning with fire-sparks, symbolled the life of the man, and from the third leaf the flame leaped up and died; and again a voice from thy breast, hollow, as if borne from a hill-top afar, made answer, 'At thine entrance to manhood life bursts into blaze, and shrivels up into ashes.' So I knew that the doom of the infant still weighed unannealed on the years of the man; and I come here to my native land as to glory and the grave. But," said the young man, with a wild enthusiasm, "still with mine links the fate which is loftiest in England; and the rill and the river shall rush in one to the Terrible Sea."

"I know not that," answered Hilda, pale, as if in awe of herself: "for never yet hath the rune, or the fount or the tomb, revealed to me clear and distinct the close of the great course of Harold; only know I through his own stars his glory and greatness; and where glory is dim, and greatness is menaced, I know it but from the stars of others, the rays of whose influence blend with his own. So long, at least, as the fair and the pure one keeps watch in the still House of Life, the dark and the troubled one cannot wholly prevail. For Edith is given to Harold as the Fylgia, that noiselessly blesses and saves: and thou—" Hilda checked herself, and lowered her hood over her face, so that it suddenly became invisible.

"And I?" asked Haco, moving near to her side.

"Away, son of Sweyn; thy feet trample the grave of the mighty dead!"

Then Hilda lingered no longer, but took her way towards the house. Haco's eye followed her in silence. The cattle, grazing in the great space of the crumbling peristyle, looked up as she passed; the watch- dogs, wandering through the star-lit columns, came snorting round their mistress. And when she had vanished within the house, Haco turned to his steed:

"What matters," he murmured, "the answer which the Vala cannot or dare not give? To me is not destined the love of woman, nor the ambition of life. All I know of human affection binds me to Harold; all I know of human ambition is to share in his fate. This love is strong as hate, and terrible as doom,—it is jealous, it admits no rival. As the shell and the sea-weed interlaced together, we are dashed on the rushing surge; whither? oh, whither?"

CHAPTER IV.

"I tell thee, Hilda," said the Earl, impatiently, "I tell thee that I renounce henceforth all faith save in Him whose ways are concealed from our eyes. Thy seid and thy galdra have not guarded me against peril, nor armed me against sin. Nay, perchance — but peace: I will no more tempt the dark art, I will no more seek to disentangle the awful truth from the juggling lie. All so foretold me I will seek to forget, — hope from no prophecy, fear from no warning. Let the soul go to the future under the shadow of God!"

"Pass on thy way as thou wilt, its goal is the same, whether seen or unmarked. Peradventure thou art wise," said the Vala, gloomily.

"For my country's sake, heaven be my witness, not my own," resumed the Earl, "I have blotted my conscience and sullied my truth. My country alone can redeem me, by taking my life as a thing hallowed evermore to her service. Selfish ambition do I lay aside, selfish power shall tempt me no more; lost is the charm that I beheld in a throne, and, save for Edith — "

"No! not even for Edith," cried the betrothed, advancing, "not even for Edith shalt thou listen to other voice than that of thy country and thy soul."

The Earl turned round abruptly, and his eyes were moist. "O Hilda," he cried, "see henceforth my only Vala; let that noble heart alone interpret to us the oracles of the future."

The next day Harold returned with Haco and a numerous train of his house-carles to the city. Their ride was as silent as that of the day before; but on reaching Southwark, Harold turned away from the bridge towards the left, gained the river-side, and dismounted at the house of one of his lithsmen (a franklin, or freed ceorl). Leaving there his horse, he summoned a boat, and, with Haco, was rowed over towards the fortified palace which then rose towards the west of London, jutting into the Thames, and which seems to have formed the outwork of the old Roman city. The palace, of remotest antiquity, and blending all work and architecture, Roman, Saxon, and Danish, had been repaired by Canute; and from a high window in the upper story, where were the royal apartments, the body of the traitor Edric Streone (the founder of the house of Godwin) had been thrown into the river.

"Whither go we, Harold?" asked the son of Sweyn.

"We go to visit the young Atheling, the natural heir to the Saxon throne," replied Harold in a firm voice. "He lodges in the old palace of our kings."

"They say in Normandy that the boy is imbecile."

"That is not true," returned Harold. "I will present thee to him,—judge."

Haco mused a moment and said:

"Methinks I divine thy purpose; is it not formed on the sudden, Harold?"

"It was the counsel of Edith," answered Harold, with evident emotion.
"And yet, if that counsel prevail, I may lose the power to soften the Church and to call her mine."

"So thou wouldest sacrifice even Edith for thy country."

"Since I have sinned, methinks I could," said the proud man humbly.

The boat shot into a little creek, or rather canal, which then ran inland, beside the black and rotting walls of the fort. The two Earlborn leapt ashore, passed under a Roman arch, entered a court the interior of which was rudely filled up by early Saxon habitations of rough timber work, already, since the time of Canute, falling into decay, (as all things did which came under the care of Edward,) and mounting a stair that ran along the outside of the house, gained a low narrow door, which stood open. In the passage within were one or two of the King's house-carles who had been assigned to the young Atheling, with liveries of blue and Danish axes, and some four or five German servitors, who had attended his father from the Emperor's court. One of these last ushered the noble Saxons into a low, forlorn ante-hall; and there, to Harold's surprise they found Alred the Archbishop of York, and three thegns of high rank, and of lineage ancient and purely Saxon.

Alred approached Harold with a faint smile on his benign face:

"Methinks, and may I think aright!—thou comest hither with the same purpose as myself, and you noble thegns."

"And that purpose?"

"Is to see and to judge calmly, if, despite his years, we may find in the descendant of the Ironsides such a prince as we may commend to our decaying King as his heir, and to the Witan as a chief fit to defend the land."

"Thou speakest the cause of my own coming. With your ears will I hear, with your eyes will I see; as ye judge, will judge I," said Harold, drawing the prelate towards the thegns, so that they might hear his answer.

The chiefs, who belonged to a party that had often opposed Godwin's House, had exchanged looks of fear and trouble when Harold entered; but at his words their frank faces showed equal surprise and pleasure.

Harold presented to them his nephew, with whose grave dignity of bearing beyond his years they were favourably impressed, though the good bishop sighed when he saw in his face the sombre beauty of the guilty sire. The group then conversed anxiously on the declining health of the King, the disturbed state of the realm, and the expediency, if possible, of uniting all suffrages in favour of the fittest successor. And in Harold's voice and manner, as in Harold's heart, there was nought that seemed conscious of his own mighty stake and just hopes in that election. But as time wore, the faces of the thegns grew overcast; proud men and great satraps [210] were they, and they liked it ill that the boy-prince kept them so long in the dismal ante-room.

At length the German officer, who had gone to announce their coming, returned; and in words, intelligible indeed from the affinity between Saxon and German, but still disagreeably foreign to English ears, requested them to follow him into the presence of the Atheling.

In a room yet retaining the rude splendour with which it had been invested by Canute, a handsome boy, about the age of thirteen or fourteen, but seeming much younger, was engaged in the construction of a stuffed bird, a lure for a young hawk that stood blindfold on its perch. The employment made so habitual a part of the serious education of youth, that the thegns smoothed their brows at the sight, and deemed the boy worthily occupied. At another end of the room, a grave Norman priest was seated at a table on which were books and writing implements; he was the tutor commissioned by Edward to teach Norman tongue and saintly lore to the Atheling. A profusion of toys strewed the floor, and some children of Edgar's own age were playing with them. His little sister Margaret [211] was seated seriously, apart from all the other children, and employed in needlework.

When Alred approached the Atheling, with a blending of reverent obeisance and paternal cordiality, the boy carelessly cried, in a barbarous jargon, half German, half Norman-French:

"There, come not too near, you scare my hawk. What are you doing? You trample my toys, which the good Norman bishop William sent me as a gift from the Duke. Art thou blind, man?"

"My son," said the prelate kindly, "these are the things of childhood —childhood ends sooner with princes than with common men. Leave thy lure and thy toys, and welcome these noble thegns, and address them, so please you, in our own Saxon tongue."

"Saxon tongue!—language of villeins! not I. Little do I know of it, save to scold a ceorl or a nurse. King Edward did not tell me to learn Saxon, but Norman! and Godfroi yonder says, that if I know Norman well, Duke William will make me his knight. But I don't desire to learn anything more to-day." And the child turned peevishly from thegn and prelate.

The three Saxon lords interchanged looks of profound displeasure and proud disgust. But Harold, with an effort over himself, approached, and said winningly:

"Edgar the Atheling, thou art not so young but thou knowest already that the great live for others. Wilt thou not be proud to live for this fair country, and these noble men, and to speak the language of Alfred the Great?"

"Alfred the Great! they always weary me with Alfred the Great," said the boy, pouting. "Alfred the Great, he is the plague of my life! if I am Atheling, men are to live for me, not I for them; and if you tease me any more, I will run away to Duke William in Rouen; Godfroi says I shall never be teased there!"

So saying, already tired of hawk and lure, the child threw himself on the floor with the other children, and snatched the toys from their hands.

The serious Margaret then rose quietly, and went to her brother, and said, in good Saxon:

"Fie! if you behave thus, I shall call you NIDDERING!" At the threat of that word, the vilest in the language — that word which the lowest ceorl would forfeit life rather than endure — a threat applied to the Atheling of England, the descendant of Saxon heroes — the three thegns drew close, and watched the boy, hoping to see that he would start to his feet with wrath and in shame.

"Call me what you will, silly sister," said the child, indifferently, "I am not so Saxon as to care for your ceorlish Saxon names."

"Enow," cried the proudest and greatest of the thegns, his very moustache curling with ire. "He who can be called niddering shall never be crowned king!"

"I don't want to be crowned king, rude man, with your laidly moustache: I want to be made knight, and have banderol and baldric. — Go away!"

"We go, son," said Alred, mournfully.

And with slow and tottering step he moved to the door; there he halted, turned back, — and the child was pointing at him in mimicry, while Godfroi, the Norman tutor, smiled as in pleasure. The prelate shook his head, and the group gained again the ante-hall.

"Fit leader of bearded men! fit king for the Saxon land!" cried a thegn. "No more of your Atheling, Alred my father!"

"No more of him, indeed!" said the prelate, mournfully. "It is but the fault of his nurture and rearing, — a neglected childhood, a Norman tutor, German hirelings. We may remould yet the pliant clay," said Harold.

"Nay," returned Alred, "no leisure for such hopes, no time to un-do what is done by circumstance, and, I fear, by nature. Ere the year is out the throne will stand empty in our halls."

"Who then," said Haco, abruptly, "who then, — (pardon the ignorance of youth wasted in captivity abroad!) who then, failing the Atheling, will save this realm from the Norman Duke, who, I know well, counts on it as the reaper on the harvest ripening to his sickle?"

"Alas, who then?" murmured Alred.

"Who then?" cried the three thegns, with one voice, "why the worthiest, the wisest, the bravest! Stand forth, Harold the Earl, Thou art the man!" And without awaiting his answer, they strode from the hall.

CHAPTER V.

Around Northampton lay the forces of Morcar, the choice of the Anglo- Dane men of Northumbria. Suddenly there was a shout as to arms from the encampment; and Morcar, the young Earl, clad in his link mail, save his helmet, came forth, and cried:

"My men are fools to look that way for a foe; yonder lies Mercia, behind it the hills of Wales. The troops that come hitherward are those which Edwin my brother brings to our aid."

Morcar's words were carried into the host by his captains and warbodes, and the shout changed from alarm into joy. As the cloud of dust through which gleamed the spears of the coming force rolled away, and lay lagging behind the march of the host, there rode forth from the van two riders. Fast and far from the rest they rode, and behind them, fast as they could, spurred two others, who bore on high, one the pennon of Mercia, one the red lion of North Wales. Right to the embankment and palisade which begirt Mortar's camp rode the riders; and the head of the foremost was bare, and the guards knew the face of Edwin the Comely, Mortar's brother. Morcar stepped down from the mound on which he stood, and the brothers embraced amidst the halloos of the forces.

"And welcome, I pray thee," said Morcar, "our kinsman Caradoc, son of
Gryffyth [212] the bold."

So Morcar reached his hand to Caradoc, stepson to his sister Aldyth, and kissed him on the brow, as was the wont of our fathers. The young and crownless prince was scarce out of boyhood, but already his name was sung by the bards, and circled in the halls of Gwynedd with the Hirlas horn; for he had harried the Saxon borders, and given to fire and sword even the fortress of Harold himself.

But while these three interchanged salutations, and ere yet the mixed Mercians and Welch had gained the encampment, from a curve in the opposite road, towards Towcester and Dunstable, broke the flash of mail like a river of light, trumpets and fifes were heard in the distance; and all in Morcar's host stood hushed but stern, gazing anxious and afar, as the coming armament swept on. And from the midst were seen the Martlets and Cross of England's king, and the Tiger heads of Harold; banners which, seen together, had planted victory on every tower, on every field, towards which they had rushed on the winds.

Retiring, then, to the central mound, the chiefs of the insurgent force held their brief council.

The two young Earls, whatever their ancestral renown, being yet new themselves to fame and to power, were submissive to the Anglo-Dane chiefs, by whom Morcar had been elected. And these, on recognising the standard of Harold, were unanimous in advice to send a peaceful deputation, setting forth their wrongs under Tostig, and the justice of their cause. "For the Earl," said Gamel Beorn (the head and front of that revolution,) is a just man, and one who would shed his own blood rather than that of any other freeborn dweller in England; and he will do us right."

"What, against his own brother?" cried Edwin.

"Against his own brother, if we convince but his reason," returned the
Anglo-Dane.

And the other chiefs nodded assent. Caradoc's fierce eyes flashed fire; but he played with his torque, and spoke not.

Meanwhile, the vanguard of the King's force had defiled under the very walls of Northampton, between the town and the insurgents; and some of the light-armed scouts who went forth from Morcar's camp to gaze on the procession, with that singular fearlessness which characterised, at that period, the rival parties in civil war, returned to say that they had seen Harold himself in the foremost line, and that he was not in mail.

This circumstance the insurgent thegns received as a good omen; and, having already agreed on the deputation, about a score of the principal thegns of the north went sedately towards the hostile lines.

By the side of Harold,—armed in mail, with his face concealed by the strange Sicilian nose-piece used then by most of the Northern nations,—had ridden Tostig, who had joined the Earl on his march, with a scanty band of some fifty or sixty of his Danish house-carles. All the men throughout broad England that he could command or bribe to his cause, were those fifty or sixty hireling Danes. And it seemed that already there was dispute between the brothers, for Harold's face was flushed, and his voice stern, as he said, "Rate me as thou wilt, brother, but I cannot advance at once to the destruction of my fellow Englishmen without summons and attempt at treaty,—as has ever been the custom of our ancient heroes and our own House."

"By all the fiends of the North?" exclaimed Tostig, "it is foul shame to talk of treaty and summons to robbers and rebels. For what art thou here but for chastisement and revenge?"

"For justice and right, Tostig."

"Ha! thou comest not, then, to aid thy brother?"

"Yes, if justice and right are, as I trust, with him."

Before Tostig could reply, a line was suddenly cleared through the armed men, and, with bare heads, and a monk lifting the rood on high, amidst the procession advanced the Northumbrian Danes.

"By the red sword of St. Olave!" cried Tostig, "yonder come the traitors, Gamel Beorn and Gloneion! You will not hear them? If so, I will not stay to listen. I have but my axe for my answer to such knaves."

"Brother, brother, those men are the most valiant and famous chiefs in thine earldom. Go, Tostig, thou art not now in the mood to hear reason. Retire into the city; summon its gates to open to the King's flag. I will hear the men."

"Beware how thou judge, save in thy brother's favour!" growled the fierce warrior; and, tossing his arm on high with a contemptuous gesture, he spurred away towards the gates.

Then Harold, dismounting, stood on the ground, under the standard of his King, and round him came several of the Saxon chiefs, who had kept aloof during the conference with Tostig.

The Northumbrians approached, and saluted the Earl with grave courtesy.

Then Gamel Beorn began. But much as Harold had feared and foreboded as to the causes of complaint which Tostig had given to the Northumbrians, all fear, all foreboding, fell short of the horrors now deliberately unfolded; not only extortion of tribute the most rapacious and illegal, but murder the fiercest and most foul. Thegns of high birth, without offence or suspicion, but who had either excited Tostig's jealousy, or resisted his exactions, had been snared under peaceful pretexts into his castle [213], and butchered in cold blood by his house-carles. The cruelties of the old heathen Danes seemed revived in the bloody and barbarous tale.

"And now," said the thegn, in conclusion, "canst thou condemn us that we rose?—no partial rising;—rose all Northumbria! At first but two hundred thegns; strong in our course, we swelled into the might of a people. Our wrongs found sympathy beyond our province, for liberty spreads over human hearts as fire over a heath. Wherever we march, friends gather round us. Thou warrest not on a handful of rebels,— half England is with us!"

"And ye,—thegns," answered Harold, "ye have ceased to war against Tostig, your Earl. Ye war now against the King and the Law. Come with your complaints to your Prince and your Witan, and, if they are just, ye are stronger than in yonder palisades and streets of steel."

"And so," said Gamel Beorn, with marked emphasis, "now thou art in England, O noble Earl,—so are we willing to come. But when thou wert absent from the land, justice seemed to abandon it to force and the battle-axe."

"I would thank you for your trust," answered Harold, deeply moved. "But justice in England rests not on the presence and life of a single man. And your speech I must not accept as a grace, for it wrongs both my King and his Council. These charges ye have made, but ye have not proved them. Armed men are not proofs; and granting that hot blood and mortal infirmity of judgment have caused Tostig to err against you and the right, think still of his qualities to reign over men whose lands, and whose rivers, lie ever exposed to the dread Northern sea- kings. Where will ye find a chief with arm as strong, and heart as dauntless? By his mother's side he is allied to your own lineage. And for the rest, if ye receive him back to his earldom, not only do I, Harold in whom you profess to trust, pledge full oblivion of the past, but I will undertake, in his name, that he shall rule you well for the future, according to the laws of King Canute."

"That will we not hear," cried the thegns, with one voice; while the tones of Gamel Beorn, rough with the rattling Danish burr, rose above all, "for we were born free. A proud and bad chief is by us not to be endured; we have learned from our ancestors to live free or die!"

A murmur, not of condemnation, at these words, was heard amongst the Saxon chiefs round Harold: and beloved and revered as he was, he felt that, had he the heart, he had scarce the power, to have coerced those warriors to march at once on their countrymen in such a cause. But foreseeing great evil in the surrender of his brother's interests, whether by lowering the King's dignity to the demands of armed force, or sending abroad in all his fierce passions a man so highly connected with Norman and Dane, so vindictive and so grasping, as Tostig, the Earl shunned further parley at that time and place. He appointed a meeting in the town with the chiefs; and requested them, meanwhile, to reconsider their demands, and at least shape them so as that they could be transmitted to the King, who was then on his way to Oxford.

It is in vain to describe the rage of Tostig, when his brother gravely repeated to him the accusations against him, and asked for his justification. Justification he could give not. His idea of law was but force, and by force alone he demanded now to be defended. Harold, then, wishing not alone to be judge in his brother's cause, referred further discussion to the chiefs of the various towns and shires, whose troops had swelled the War-Fyrd; and to them he bade Tostig plead his cause.

Vain as a woman, while fierce as a tiger, Tostig assented, and in that assembly he rose, his gonna all blazing with crimson and gold, his hair all curled and perfumed as for a banquet; and such, in a half- barbarous day, the effect of person, especially when backed by warlike renown, that the Proceres were half disposed to forget, in admiration of the earl's surpassing beauty of form, the dark tales of his hideous guilt. But his passions hurrying him away ere he had gained the middle of his discourse, so did his own relation condemn himself, so clear became his own tyrannous misdeeds, that the Englishmen murmured aloud their disgust, and their impatience would not suffer him to close.

"Enough," cried Vebba, the blunt thegn from Saxon Kent; "it is plain that neither King nor Witan can replace thee in thine earldom. Tell us not farther of these atrocities; or by're Lady, if the Northumbrians had chased thee not, we would."

"Take treasure and ship, and go to Baldwin in Flanders," said Thorold, a great Anglo-Dane from Lincolnshire, "for even Harold's name can scarce save thee from outlawry."

Tostig glared round on the assembly, and met but one common expression in the face of all.

"These are thy henchmen, Harold!" he said through his gnashing teeth, without vouchsafing farther word, strode from the council-hall.

That evening he left the town and hurried to tell to Edward the tale that had so miscarried with the chiefs. The next day, the Northumbrian delegates were heard; and they made the customary proposition in those cases of civil differences, to refer all matters to the King and the Witan; each party remaining under arms meanwhile.

This was finally acceded to. Harold repaired to Oxford, where the King (persuaded to the journey by Alred, foreseeing what would come to pass) had just arrived.

CHAPTER VI.

The Witan was summoned in haste. Thither came the young earls Morcar and Edwin, but Caradoc, chafing at the thought of peace, retired into Wales with his wild band.

Now, all the great chiefs, spiritual and temporal, assembled in Oxford for the decree of that Witan on which depended the peace of England. The imminence of the time made the concourse of members entitled to vote in the assembly even larger than that which had met for the inlawry of Godwin. There was but one thought uppermost in the minds of men, to which the adjustment of an earldom, however mighty, was comparatively insignificant—viz., the succession of the kingdom. That thought turned instinctively and irresistibly to Harold.

The evident and rapid decay of the King; the utter failure of all male heir in the House of Cerdic, save only the boy Edgar; whose character (which throughout life remained puerile and frivolous) made the minority which excluded him from the throne seem cause rather for rejoicing than grief: and whose rights, even by birth, were not acknowledged by the general tenor of the Saxon laws, which did not recognize as heir to the crown the son of a father who had not himself been crowned [214];—forebodings of coming evil and danger, originating in Edward's perturbed visions; revivals of obscure and till then forgotten prophecies, ancient as the days of Merlin; rumours, industriously fomented into certainty by Haco, whose whole soul seemed devoted to Harold's cause, of the intended claim of the Norman Count to the throne;—all concurred to make the election of a man matured in camp and council, doubly necessary to the safety of the realm.

Warm favourers, naturally, of Harold, were the genuine Saxon population, and a large part of the Anglo-Danish—all the thegns in his vast earldom of Wessex, reaching to the southern and western coasts, from Sandwich and the mouth of the Thames to the Land's End in Cornwall; and including the free men of Kent, whose inhabitants even from the days of Caesar had been considered in advance of the rest of the British population, and from the days of Hengist had exercised an influence that nothing save the warlike might of the Anglo-Danes counterbalanced. With Harold, too, were many of the thegns from his earlier earldom of East Anglia, comprising the county of Essex, great part of Hertfordshire, and so reaching into Cambridge, Huntingdon, Norfolk, and Ely. With him, were all the wealth, intelligence, and power of London, and most of the trading towns; with him all the veterans of the armies he had led; with him too, generally throughout the empire, was the force, less distinctly demarked, of public and national feeling.

Even the priests, save those immediately about the court, forgot, in the exigency of the time, their ancient and deep-rooted dislike to Godwin's House; they remembered, at least, that Harold had never, in foray or feud, plundered a single convent; or in peace, and through plot, appropriated to himself a single hide of Church land; and that was more than could have been said of any other earl of the age—even of Leofric the Holy. They caught, as a Church must do, when so intimately, even in its illiterate errors, allied with the people as the old Saxon Church was, the popular enthusiasm. Abbot combined with thegn in zeal for Earl Harold.

The only party that stood aloof was the one that espoused the claims of the young sons of Algar. But this party was indeed most formidable; it united all. the old friends of the virtuous Leofric, of the famous Siward; it had a numerous party even in East Anglia (in which earldom Algar had succeeded Harold); it comprised nearly all the thegns in Mercia (the heart of the country) and the population of Northumbria; and it involved in its wide range the terrible Welch on the one hand, and the Scottish domain of the sub-king Malcolm, himself a Cumbrian, on the other, despite Malcolm's personal predilections for Tostig, to whom he was strongly attached. But then the chiefs of this party, while at present they stood aloof, were all, with the exception perhaps of the young earls themselves, disposed, on the slightest encouragement, to blend their suffrage with the friends of Harold; and his praise was as loud on their lips as on those of the Saxons from Kent, or the burghers from London. All factions, in short, were willing, in this momentous crisis, to lay aside old dissensions; it depended upon the conciliation of the Northumbrians, upon a fusion between the friends of Harold and the supporters of the young sons of Algar, to form such a concurrence of interests as must inevitably bear Harold to the throne of the empire.

Meanwhile, the Earl himself wisely and patriotically deemed it right to remain neuter in the approaching decision between Tostig and the young earls. He could not be so unjust and so mad as to urge to the utmost (and risk in the urging) his party influence on the side of oppression and injustice, solely for the sake of his brother; nor, on the other, was it decorous or natural to take part himself against Tostig; nor could he, as a statesman, contemplate without anxiety and alarm the transfer of so large a portion of the realm to the vice- kingship of the sons of his old foe—rivals to his power, at the very time when, even for the sake of England alone, that power should be the most solid and compact.

But the final greatness of a fortunate man is rarely made by any violent effort of his own. He has sown the seeds in the time foregone, and the ripe time brings up the harvest. His fate seems taken out of his own control: greatness seems thrust upon him. He has made himself, as it were, a want to the nation, a thing necessary to it; he has identified himself with his age, and in the wreath or the crown on his brow, the age itself seems to put forth its flower.

Tostig, lodging apart from Harold in a fort near the gate of Oxford, took slight pains to conciliate foes or make friends; trusting rather to his representations to Edward, (who was wroth with the rebellious House of Algar,) of the danger of compromising the royal dignity by concessions to armed insurgents.

It was but three days before that for which the Witan was summoned; most of its members had already assembled in the city; and Harold, from the window of the monastery in which he lodged, was gazing thoughtfully into the streets below, where, with the gay dresses of the thegns and cnehts, blended the grave robes of ecclesiastic and youthful scholar;—for to that illustrious university (pillaged the persecuted by the sons of Canute), Edward had, to his honour, restored the schools,—when Haco entered, and announced to him that a numerous body of thegns and prelates, headed by Alred, Archbishop of York, craved an audience.

"Knowest thou the cause, Haco?"

The youth's cheek was yet more pale than usual, as he answered slowly:

"Hilda's prophecies are ripening into truths."

The Earl started, and his old ambition reviving, flushed on his brow, and sparkled from his eye—he checked the joyous emotion, and bade Haco briefly admit the visitors.

They came in, two by two,—a body so numerous that they filled the ample chamber; and Harold, as he greeted each, beheld the most powerful lords of the land—the highest dignitaries of the Church—and, oft and frequent, came old foe by the side or trusty friend. They all paused at the foot of the narrow dais on which Harold stood, and Alred repelled by a gesture his invitation to the foremost to mount the platform.

Then Alred began an harangue, simple and earnest. He described briefly the condition of the country; touched with grief and with feeling on the health of the King, and the failure of Cerdic's line. He stated honestly his own strong wish, if possible, to have concentrated the popular suffrages on the young Atheling; and under the emergence of the case, to have waived the objection to his immature years. But as distinctly and emphatically he stated, that that hope and intent he had now formally abandoned, and that there was but one sentiment on the subject with all the chiefs and dignitaries of the realm.

"Wherefore," continued he, "after anxious consultations with each other, those whom you see around have come to you: yea, to you, Earl Harold, we offer our hands and hearts to do our best to prepare for you the throne on the demise of Edward, and to seat you thereon as firmly as ever sate King of England and son of Cerdic; — knowing that in you, and in you alone, we find the man who reigns already in the English heart; to whose strong arm we can trust the defence of our land; to whose just thoughts, our laws. — As I speak, so think we all!"

With downcast eyes, Harold heard; and but by a slight heaving of his breast under his crimson robe, could his emotion be seen. But as soon as the approving murmur that succeeded the prelate's speech, had closed, he lifted his head, and answered:

"Holy father, and you, Right Worthy my fellow-thegns, if ye could read my heart at this moment, believe that you would not find there the vain joy of aspiring man, when the greatest of earthly prizes is placed within his reach. There, you would see, with deep and wordless gratitude for your trust and your love, grave and solemn solicitude, earnest desire to divest my decision of all mean thought of self, and judge only whether indeed, as king or as subject, I can best guard the weal of England. Pardon me, then, if I answer you not as ambition alone would answer; neither deem me insensible to the glorious lot of presiding, under heaven, and by the light of our laws, over the destinies of the English realm, — if I pause to weigh well the responsibilities incurred, and the obstacles to be surmounted. There is that on my mind that I would fain unbosom, not of a nature to discuss in an assembly so numerous, but which I would rather submit to a chosen few whom you yourselves may select to hear me, in whose cool wisdom, apart from personal love to me, ye may best confide; — your most veteran thegns, your most honoured prelates: To them will I speak, to them make clean my bosom; and to their answer, their counsels, will I in all things defer: whether with loyal heart to serve another, whom, hearing me, they may decide to choose; or to fit my soul to bear, not unworthily, the weight of a kingly crown."

Alred lifted his mild eyes to Harold, and there were both pity and approval in his gaze, for he divined the Earl.

"Thou hast chosen the right course, my son; and we will retire at once, and elect those with whom thou mayest freely confer, and by whose judgment thou mayest righteously abide."

The prelate turned, and with him went the conclave. Left alone with Haco, the last said, abruptly:

"Thou wilt not be so indiscreet, O Harold, as to confess thy compelled oath to the fraudful Norman?"

"That is my design," replied Harold, coldly.

The son of Sweyn began to remonstrate, but the Earl cut him short.

"If the Norman say that he has been deceived in Harold, never so shall say the men of England. Leave me. I know not why, Haco, but in thy presence, at times, there is a glamour as strong as in the spells of Hilda. Go, dear boy; the fault is not in thee, but in the superstitious infirmities of a man who hath once lowered, or, it may be, too highly strained, his reason to the things of a haggard fancy. Go! and send to me my brother Gurth. I would have him alone of my House present at this solemn crisis of its fate."

Haco bowed his head, and went.

In a few moments more, Gurth came in. To this pure and spotless spirit Harold had already related the events of his unhappy visit to the Norman; and he felt, as the young chief pressed his hand, and looked on him with his clear and loving eyes, as if Honour made palpable stood by his side.

Six of the ecclesiastics, most eminent for Church learning, — small as was that which they could boast, compared with the scholars of Normandy and the Papal States, but at least more intelligent and more free from mere formal monasticism than most of their Saxon contemporaries, — and six of the chiefs most renowned for experience in war or council, selected under the sagacious promptings of Alred, accompanied that prelate to the presence of the Earl.

"Close, thou! close! close! Gurth," whispered Harold "for this is a confession against man's pride, and sorely doth it shame; — so that I would have thy bold sinless heart beating near to mine."

Then, leaning his arm upon his brother's shoulder, and in a voice, the first tones of which, as betraying earnest emotion, irresistibly chained and affected his noble audience, Harold began his tale.

Various were the emotions, though all more akin to terror than repugnance, with which the listeners heard the Earl's plain and candid recital.

Among the lay-chiefs the impression made by the compelled oath was comparatively slight: for it was the worst vice of the Saxon laws, to entangle all charges, from the smallest to the greatest, in a reckless multiplicity of oaths [215], to the grievous loosening of the bonds of truth: and oaths then had become almost as much mere matter of legal form, as certain oaths—bad relic of those times!—still existing in our parliamentary and collegiate proceedings, are deemed by men, not otherwise dishonourable, even now. And to no kind of oath was more latitude given than to such as related to fealty to a chief: for these, in the constant rebellions which happened year after year, were openly violated, and without reproach. Not a sub-king in Wales who harried the border, not an earl who raised banner against the Basileus of Britain, but infringed his oath to be good man and true to the lord paramount; and even William the Norman himself never found his oath of fealty stand in the way, whenever he deemed it right and expedient to take arms against his suzerain of France.

On the churchmen the impression was stronger and more serious: not that made by the oath itself, but by the relics on which the hand had been laid. They looked at each other, doubtful and appalled, when the Earl ceased his tale; while only among the laymen circled a murmur of mingled wrath at William's bold design on their native land, and of scorn at the thought that an oath, surprised and compelled, should be made the instrument of treason to a whole people.

"Thus," said Harold, after a pause, "thus have I made clear to you my conscience, and revealed to you the only obstacle between your offers and my choice. From the keeping of an oath so extorted, and so deadly to England, this venerable prelate and mine own soul have freed me. Whether as king or as subject, I shall alike revere the living and their long posterity more than the dead men's bones, and, with sword and with battle-axe, hew out against the invader my best atonement for the lip's weakness and the heart's desertion. But whether, knowing what hath passed, ye may not deem it safer for the land to elect another king,—this it is which, free and fore-thoughtful of every chance, ye should now decide."

With these words he stepped from the dais, and retired into the oratory that adjoined the chamber, followed by Gurth. The eyes of the priests then turned to Alred, and to them the prelate spoke as he had done before to Harold;—he distinguished between the oath and its fulfilment—between the lesser sin and the greater—the one which the Church could absolve—the one which no Church had the right to exact, and which, if fulfilled, no penance could expiate. He owned frankly, nevertheless, that it was the difficulties so created, that had made him incline to the Atheling;—but, convinced of that prince's incapacity, even in the most ordinary times, to rule Eng-land, he shrank yet more from such a choice, when the swords of the Norman were already sharpening for contest. Finally he said, "If a man as fit to defend us as Harold can be found, let us prefer him: if not——"

"There is no other man!" cried the thegns with one voice. "And," said a wise old chief, "had Harold sought to play a trick to secure the throne, he could not have devised one more sure than the tale he hath now told us. What! just when we are most assured that the doughtiest and deadliest foe that our land can brave, waits but for Edward's death to enforce on us a stranger's yoke—what! shall we for that very reason deprive ourselves of the only man able to resist him? Harold hath taken an oath! God wot, who among us have not taken some oath at law for which they have deemed it meet after-wards to do a penance, or endow a convent? The wisest means to strengthen Harold against that oath, is to show the moral impossi-bility of fulfilling it, by placing him on the throne. The best proof we can give to this insolent Norman that England is not for prince to leave, or subject to barter, is to choose solemnly in our Witan the very chief whom his frauds prove to us that he fears the most. Why, William would laugh in his own sleeve to summon a king to de-scend from his throne to do him the homage which that king, in the different capacity of subject, had (we will grant, even willingly) promised to render."

This speech spoke all the thoughts of the laymen, and, with Alred's previous remarks, reassured all the ecclesiastics. They were easily induced to believe that the usual Church penances, and ample Church gifts, would suffice for the insult offered to the relics: and,—if they in so grave a case outstripped, in absolution, an authority amply sufficing for all ordinary matters,—Harold, as king, might easily gain from the Pope himself that full pardon and shrift, which as mere earl, against the Prince of the Normans, he would fail of obtaining.

These or similar reflections soon terminated the suspense of the select council; and Alred sought the Earl in the oratory, to summon him back to the conclave. The two brothers were kneeling side by side before the little altar; and there was something inexpressibly touching in their humble attitudes, their clasped supplicating hands, in that moment when the crown of England rested above their House.

The brothers rose, and at Alred's sign followed the prelate into the council-room. Alred briefly communicated the result of the conference; and with an aspect, and in a tone, free alike from triumph and indecision, Harold replied:

"As ye will, so will I. Place me only where I can most serve the common cause. Remain you now, knowing my secret, a chosen and standing council: too great is my personal stake in this matter to allow my mind to be unbiassed; judge ye, then, and decide for me in all things: your minds should be calmer and wiser than mine; in all things I will abide by your counsel; and thus I accept the trust of a nation's freedom."

Each thegn then put his hand into Harold's, and called himself Harold's man.

"Now, more than ever," said the wise old thegn who had before spoken, "will it be needful to heal all dissension in the kingdom—to reconcile with us Mercia and Northumbria, and make the kingdom one against the foe. You, as Tostig's brother, have done well to abstain from active interference; you do well to leave it to us to negotiate the necessary alliance between all brave and good men."

"And to that end, as imperative for the public weal, you consent," said Alred, thoughtfully, "to abide by our advice, whatever it be?"

"Whatever it be, so that it serve England," answered the Earl.

A smile, somewhat sad, flitted over the prelate's pale lips, and Harold was once more alone with Gurth.

CHAPTER VII.

The soul of all council and cabal on behalf of Harold, which has led to the determination of the principal chiefs, and which now succeeded it — was Haco.

His rank as son of Sweyn, the first-born of Godwin's house — a rank which might have authorised some pretensions on his own part, gave him all field for the exercise of an intellect singularly keen and profound. Accustomed to an atmosphere of practical state-craft in the Norman court, with faculties sharpened from boyhood by vigilance and meditation, he exercised an extraordinary influence over the simple understandings of the homely clergy and the uncultured thegns. Impressed with the conviction of his early doom, he felt no interest in the objects of others; but equally believing that whatever of bright, and brave, and glorious, in his brief, condemned career, was to be reflected on him from the light of Harold's destiny, the sole desire of a nature, which, under other auspices, would have been intensely daring and ambitious, was to administer to Harold's greatness. No prejudice, no principle, stood in the way of this dreary enthusiasm. As a father, himself on the brink of the grave, schemes for the worldly grandeur of the son, in which he confounds and melts his own life, so this sombre and predestined man, dead to earth and to joy and the emotions of the heart, looked beyond his own tomb, to that existence in which he transferred and carried on his ambition.

If the leading agencies of Harold's memorable career might be, as it were, symbolised and allegorised, by the living beings with which it was connected—as Edith was the representative of stainless Truth—as Gurth was the type of dauntless Duty—as Hilda embodied aspiring Imagination—so Haco seemed the personation of Worldly Wisdom. And cold in that worldly wisdom Haco laboured on, now conferring with Alred and the partisans of Harold; now closeted with Edwin and Morcar; now gliding from the chamber of the sick King.—That wisdom foresaw all obstacles, smoothed all difficulties; ever calm, never resting; marshalling and harmonising the things to be, like the ruthless hand of a tranquil fate. But there was one with whom Haco was more often than with all others—one whom the presence of Harold had allured to that anxious scene of intrigue, and whose heart leapt high at the hopes whispered from the smileless lips of Haco.

CHAPTER VIII.

It was the second day after that which assured him the allegiance of the thegns, that a message was brought to Harold from the Lady Aldyth. She was in Oxford, at a convent, with her young daughter by the Welch King; she prayed him to visit her. The Earl, whose active mind, abstaining from the intrigues around him, was delivered up to the thoughts, restless and feverish, which haunt the repose of all active minds, was not unwilling to escape awhile from himself. He went to Aldyth. The royal widow had laid by the signs of mourning; she was dressed with the usual stately and loose-robed splendour of Saxon matrons, and all the proud beauty of her youth was restored to her cheek. At her feet was that daughter who afterwards married the Fleance so familiar to us in Shakespeare, and became the ancestral mother of those Scottish kings who had passed, in pale shadows, across the eyes of Macbeth [216]; by the side of that child, Harold to his surprise saw the ever ominous face of Haco.

But proud as was Aldyth, all pride seemed humbled into woman's sweeter emotions at the sight of the Earl, and she was at first unable to command words to answer his greeting.

Gradually, however, she warmed into cordial confidence. She touched lightly on her past sorrows; she permitted it to be seen that her lot with the fierce Gryffyth had been one not more of public calamity than of domestic grief, and that in the natural awe and horror which the murder of her lord had caused, she felt rather for the ill-starred king than the beloved spouse. She then passed to the differences still existing between her house and Harold's, and spoke well and wisely of the desire of the young Earls to conciliate his grace and favour.

While thus speaking, Morcar and Edwin, as if accidentally, entered, and their salutations of Harold were such as became their relative positions; reserved, not distant—respectful, not servile. With the delicacy of high natures, they avoided touching on the cause before the Witan (fixed for the morrow), on which depended their earldoms or their exile.

Harold was pleased by their bearing, and attracted towards them by the memory of the affectionate words that had passed between him and Leofric, their illustrious grandsire, over his father's corpse. He thought then of his own prayer: "Let there be peace between thine and mine!" and looking at their fair and stately youth, and noble carriage, he could not but feel that the men of Northumbria and of Mercia had chosen well. The discourse, however, was naturally brief, since thus made general; the visit soon ceased, and the brothers attended Harold to the door with the courtesy of the times. Then Haco said, with that faint movement of the lips which was his only approach to a smile:

"Will ye not, noble thegns, give your hands to my kinsman?"

"Surely," said Edwin, the handsomer and more gentle of the two, and who, having a poet's nature, felt a poet's enthusiasm for the gallant deeds even of a rival,—"surely, if the Earl will accept the hands of those who trust never to be compelled to draw sword against England's hero."

Harold stretched forth his hand in reply, and that cordial and immemorial pledge of our national friendships was interchanged.

Gaining the street, Harold said to his nephew:

"Standing as I do towards the young Earls, that appeal of thine had been better omitted."

"Nay," answered Haco; "their cause is already prejudged in their favour. And thou must ally thyself with the heirs of Leofric, and the successors of Siward."

Harold made no answer. There was something in the positive tone of this beardless youth that displeased him; but he remembered that Haco was the son of Sweyn, Godwin's first-born, and that, but for Sweyn's crimes, Haco might have held the place in England he held himself, and looked to the same august destinies beyond.

In the evening a messenger from the Roman house arrived, with two letters for Harold; one from Hilda, that contained but these words: "Again peril menaces thee, but in the shape of good. Beware! and, above all, of the evil that wears the form of wisdom."

The other letter was from Edith; it was long for the letters of that age, and every sentence spoke a heart wrapped in his.

Reading the last, Hilda's warnings were forgotten. The picture of Edith—the prospect of a power that might at last effect their union, and reward her long devotion—rose before him, to the exclusion of wilder fancies and loftier hopes; and his sleep that night was full of youthful and happy dreams.

The next day the Witan met. The meeting was less stormy than had been expected; for the minds of most men were made up, and so far as Tostig was interested, the facts were too evident and notorious, the witnesses too numerous, to leave any option to the judges. Edward, on whom alone Tostig had relied, had already, with his ordinary vacillation, been swayed towards a right decision, partly by the counsels of Alred and his other prelates, and especially by the representations of Haco, whose grave bearing and profound dissimulation had gained a singular influence over the formal and melancholy King.

By some previous compact or understanding between the opposing parties, there was no attempt, however, to push matters against the offending Tostig to vindictive extremes. There was no suggestion of outlawry, or punishment, beyond the simple deprivation of the earldom he had abused. And in return for this moderation on the one side, the other agreed to support and ratify the new election of the Northumbrians. Morcar was thus formally invested with the vice- kingship of that great realm; while Edwin was confirmed in the earldom of the principal part of Mercia.

On the announcement of these decrees, which were received with loud applause by all the crowd assembled to hear them, Tostig, rallying round him his house-carles, left the town. He went first to Githa, with whom his wife had sought refuge, and, after a long conference with his mother, he, and his haughty Countess, journeyed to the sea- coast, and took ship for Flanders.

CHAPTER IX.

Gurth and Harold were seated in close commune in the Earl's chamber, at an hour long after the complin (or second vespers), when Alred entered unexpectedly. The old man's face was unusually grave, and Harold's penetrating eye saw that he was gloomy with some matters of great moment.

"Harold," said the prelate, seating himself, "the hour has come to test thy truth, when thou saidst that thou wert ready to make all sacrifice to thy land, and further, that thou wouldst abide by the counsel of those free from thy passions, and looking on thee only as the instrument of England's weal."

"Speak on, father," said Harold, turning somewhat pale at the solemnity of the address; "I am ready, if the council so desire, to remain a subject, and aid in the choice of a worthier king."

"Thou divinest me ill," answered Alred; "I do not call on thee to lay aside the crown, but to crucify the heart. The decree of the Witan assigns Mercia and Northumbria to the sons of Algar. The old demarcations of the heptarchy, as thou knowest, are scarce worn out; it is even now less one monarchy, than various states retaining their own laws, and inhabited by different races, who under the subkings, called earls, acknowledge a supreme head in the Basileus of Britain. Mercia hath its March law and its prince; Northumbria its Dane law and its leader. To elect a king without civil war, these realms, for so they are, must unite with and sanction the Witans elsewhere held. Only thus can the kingdom be firm against foes without and anarchy within; and the more so, from the alliance between the new earls of those great provinces and the House of Gryffyth, which still lives in Caradoc his son. What if at Edward's death Mercia and Northumbria refuse to sanction thy accession? What if, when all our force were needed against the Norman, the Welch broke loose from their hills, and the Scots from their moors! Malcolm of Cumbria, now King of Scotland, is Tostig's dearest friend, while his people side with Morcar. Verily these are dangers enow for a new king, even if William's sword slept in its sheath."

"Thou speakest the words of wisdom," said Harold, "but I knew beforehand that he who wears a crown must abjure repose."

"Not so; there is one way, and but one, to reconcile all England to thy dominion—to win to thee not the cold neutrality but the eager zeal of Mercia and Northumbria; to make the first guard thee from the Welch, the last be thy rampart against the Scot. In a word, thou must ally thyself with the blood of these young earls; thou must wed with Aldyth their sister."

The Earl sprang to his feet aghast.

"No—no!" he exclaimed; "not that!—any sacrifice but that!—rather forfeit the throne than resign the heart that leans on mine! Thou knowest my pledge to Edith, my cousin; pledge hallowed by the faith of long years. No—no, have mercy—human mercy; I can wed no other!—any sacrifice but that!"

The good prelate, though not unprepared for this burst, was much moved by its genuine anguish; but, steadfast to his purpose, he resumed:

"Alas, my son, so say we all in the hour of trial—any sacrifice but that which duty and Heaven ordain. Resign the throne thou canst not, or thou leavest the land without a ruler, distracted by rival claims and ambitions, an easy prey to the Norman. Resign thy human affections thou canst and must; and the more, O Harold, that even if duty compelled not this new alliance, the old tie is one of sin, which, as king, and as high example in high place to all men, thy conscience within, and the Church without, summon thee to break. How purify the erring lives of the churchman, if thyself a rebel to the Church? and if thou hast thought that thy power as king might prevail on the Roman Pontiff to grant dispensation for wedlock within the degrees, and that so thou mightest legally confirm thy now illegal troth; bethink thee well, thou hast a more dread and urgent boon now to ask—in absolution from thine oath to William. Both prayers, surely, our Roman father will not grant. Wilt thou choose that which absolves from sin, or that which consults but thy carnal affections?"

Harold covered his face with his hands, and groaned aloud in his strong agony.

"Aid me, Gurth," cried Alred, "thou, sinless and spotless; thou, in whose voice a brother's love can blend with a Christian's zeal; aid me, Gurth, to melt the stubborn, but to comfort the human, heart."

Then Gurth, with a strong effort over himself, knelt by Harold's side, and in strong simple language, backed the representations of the priest. In truth, all argument drawn from reason, whether in the state of the land, or the new duties to which Harold was committed, were on the one side, and unanswerable; on the other, was but that mighty resistance which love opposes ever to reason. And Harold continued to murmur, while his hands concealed his face.

"Impossible!—she who trusted, who trusts—who so loves—she whose whole youth hath been consumed in patient faith in me!—Resign her! and for another! I cannot—I cannot. Take from me the throne!—Oh vain heart of man, that so long desired its own curse!—Crown the Atheling; my manhood shall defend his youth.—But not this offering! No, no—I will not!"

It were tedious to relate the rest of that prolonged and agitatated conference. All that night, till the last stars waned, and the bells of prime were heard from church and convent, did the priest and the brother alternately plead and remonstrate, chide and soothe; and still Harold's heart clung to Edith's, with its bleeding roots. At length they, perhaps not unwisely, left him to himself; and as, whispering low their hopes and their fears of the result of the self-conflict, they went forth from the convent, Haco joined them in the courtyard, and while his cold mournful eye scanned the faces of priest and brother, he asked them "how they had sped?"

Alred shook his head and answered:

"Man's heart is more strong in the flesh than true to the spirit."

"Pardon me, father," said Haco, "if I suggest that your most eloquent and persuasive ally in this, were Edith herself. Start not so incredulously; it is because she loves the Earl more than her own life, that—once show her that the Earl's safety, greatness, honour, duty, lie in release from his troth to her—that nought save his erring love resists your counsels and his country's claims—and Edith's voice will have more power than yours."

The virtuous prelate, more acquainted with man's selfishness than woman's devotion, only replied by an impatient gesture. But Gurth, lately wedded to a woman worthy of him, said gravely:

"Haco speaks well, my father; and methinks it is due to both that Edith should not, unconsulted, be abandoned by him for whom she has abjured all others; to whom she has been as devoted in heart as if sworn wife already. Leave we awhile my brother, never the slave of passion, and with whom England must at last prevail over all selfish thought; and ride we at once to tell to Edith what we have told to him; or rather—woman can best in such a case speak to woman—let us tell all to our Lady—Edward's wife, Harold's sister, and Edith's holy godmother—and abide by her counsel. On the third day we shall return."

"Go we so charged, noble Gurth," said Haco, observing the prelate's reluctant countenance, "and leave we our reverend father to watch over the Earl's sharp struggle."

"Thou speakest well, my son," said the prelate, "and thy mission suits the young and the layman, better than the old and the priest."

"Let us go, Haco," said Gurth, briefly. "Deep, sore, and lasting, is the wound I inflict on the brother of my love; and my own heart bleeds in his; but he himself hath taught me to hold England as a Roman held Rome."

CHAPTER X.

It is the nature of that happiness which we derive from our affections to be calm; its immense influence upon our outward life is not known till it is troubled or withdrawn. By placing his heart at peace, man leaves vent to his energies and passions, and permits their current to flow towards the aims and objects which interest labour or arouse ambition. Thus absorbed in the occupation without, he is lulled into a certain forgetfulness of the value of that internal repose which gives health and vigour to the faculties he employs abroad. But once mar this scarce felt, almost invisible harmony, and the discord extends to the remotest chords of our active being. Say to the busiest man whom thou seest in mart, camp, or senate, who seems to thee all intent upon his worldly schemes, "Thy home is reft from thee — thy household gods are shattered — that sweet noiseless content in the regular mechanism of the springs, which set the large wheels of thy soul into movement, is thine nevermore!" — and straightway all exertion seems robbed of its object — all aim of its alluring charm. "Othello's occupation is gone!" With a start, that man will awaken from the sunlit visions of noontide ambition, and exclaim in his desolation anguish, "What are all the rewards to my labour now thou hast robbed me of repose? How little are all the gains wrung from strife, in a world of rivals and foes, compared to the smile whose sweetness I knew not till it was lost; and the sense of security from mortal ill which I took from the trust and sympathy of love?"

Thus was it with Harold in that bitter and terrible crisis of his fate. This rare and spiritual love, which had existed on hope which had never known fruition, had become the subtlest, the most exquisite part of his being; this love, to the full and holy possession of which, every step in his career seemed to advance him, was it now to be evermore reft from his heart, his existence, at the very moment when he had deemed himself most secure of its rewards—when he most needed its consolations? Hitherto, in that love he had lived in the future—he had silenced the voice of the turbulent human passion by the whisper of the patient angel, "A little while yet, and thy bride sits beside thy throne!" Now what was that future! how joyless! how desolate! The splendour vanished from Ambition—the glow from the face of Fame—the sense of Duty remained alone to counteract the pleadings of Affection; but Duty, no longer dressed in all the gorgeous colourings it took before from glory and power—Duty stern, and harsh, and terrible, as the iron frown of a Grecian Destiny.

And thus, front to front with that Duty, he sate alone one evening, while his lips murmured, "Oh fatal voyage, oh lying truth in the hell- born prophecy! this, then, this was the wife my league with the Norman was to win to my arms!" In the streets below were heard the tramp of busy feet hurrying homeward, and the confused uproar of joyous wassail from the various resorts of entertainment crowded by careless revellers. And the tread of steps mounted the stairs without his door, and there paused;—and there was the murmur of two voices without; one the clear voice of Gurth,—one softer and more troubled. The Earl lifted his head from his bosom, and his heart beat quick at the faint and scarce heard sound of that last voice. The door opened gently, gently: a form entered, and halted on the shadow of the threshold; the door closed again by a hand from without. The Earl rose to his feet, tremulously, and the next moment Edith was at his knees; her hood thrown back, her face upturned to his, bright with unfaded beauty, serene with the grandeur of self-martyrdom.

"O Harold!" she exclaimed, "dost thou remember that in the old time I said, 'Edith had loved thee less, if thou hadst not loved England more than Edith?' Recall, recall those words. And deemest thou now that I, who have gazed for years into thy clear soul, and learned there to sun my woman's heart in the light of all glories native to noblest man, deemest thou, O Harold, that I am weaker now than then, when I scarce knew what England and glory were?"

"Edith, Edith, what wouldst thou say?—What knowest thou?—Who hath told thee?—What led thee hither, to take part against thyself?"

"It matters not who told me; I know all. What led me? Mine own soul, and mine own love!" Springing to her feet and clasping his hand in both hers, while she looked into his face, she resumed: "I do not say to thee, 'Grieve not to part;' for I know too well thy faith, thy tenderness—thy heart, so grand and so soft. But I do say, 'Soar above thy grief, and be more than man for the sake of men!' Yes, Harold, for this last time I behold thee. I clasp thy hand, I lean on thy heart, I hear its beating, and I shall go hence without a tear."

"It cannot, it shall not be!" exclaimed Harold, passionately. "Thou deceivest thyself in the divine passion of the hour: thou canst not foresee the utterness of the desolation to which thou wouldst doom thy life. We were betrothed to each other by ties strong as those of the Church,—over the grave of the dead, under the vault of heaven, in the form of ancestral faith! The bond cannot be broken. If England demands me, let England take me with the ties it were unholy, even for her sake, to rend!"

"Alas, alas!" faltered Edith, while the flush on her cheek sank into mournful paleness. "It is not as thou sayest. So has thy love sheltered me from the world—so utter was my youth's ignorance or my heart's oblivion of the stern laws of man, that when it pleased thee that we should love each other, I could not believe that that love was sin; and that it was sin hitherto I will not think;—now it hath become one."

"No, no!" cried Harold; all the eloquence on which thousands had hung, thrilled and spell-bound, deserting him in that hour of need, and leaving to him only broken exclamations,—fragments, in each of which has his heart itself seemed shivered; "no, no,—not sin!—sin only to forsake thee.—Hush! hush!—This is a dream—wait till we wake! True heart! noble soul!—I will not part from thee!"

"But I from thee! And rather than thou shouldst be lost for my sake— the sake of woman—to honour and conscience, and all for which thy sublime life sprang from the hands of Nature—if not the cloister, may I find the grave!—Harold, to the last let me be worthy of thee; and feel, at least, that if not thy wife—that bright, that blessed fate not mine! — still, remembering Edith, just men may say, 'She would not have dishonoured the hearth of Harold!'"

"Dost thou know," said the Earl, striving to speak calmly, "dost thou know that it is not only to resign thee that they demand — that it is to resign thee, and for another?"

"I know it," said Edith; and two burning tears, despite her strong and preternatural self-exaltation, swelled from the dark fringe, and rolled slowly down the colourless cheek, as she added, with proud voice, "I know it: but that other is not Aldyth, it is England! In her, in Aldyth, behold the dear cause of thy native land; with her enweave the love which thy native land should command. So thinking, thou art reconciled, and I consoled. It is not for woman that thou desertest Edith."

"Hear, and take from those lips the strength and the valour that belong to the name of Hero!" said a deep and clear voice behind; and Gurth, — who, whether distrusting the result of an interview so prolonged, or tenderly desirous to terminate its pain, had entered unobserved, — approached, and wound his arm caressingly round his brother. "Oh, Harold!" he said, "dear to me as the drops in my heart is my young bride, newly wed; but if for one tithe of the claims that now call thee to the torture and trial — yea, if but for one hour of good service to freedom and law — I would consent without a groan to behold her no more. And if men asked me how I could so conquer man's affections, I would point to thee, and say, 'So Harold taught my youth by his lessons, and my manhood by his life.' Before thee, visible, stand Happiness and Love, but with them, Shame; before thee, invisible, stands Woe, but with Woe are England and eternal Glory! Choose between them."

"He hath chosen," said Edith, as Harold turned to the wall, and leaned against it, hiding his face; then, approaching softly, she knelt, lifted to her lips the hem of his robe, and kissed it with devout passion.

Harold turned suddenly, and opened his arms. Edith resisted not that mute appeal; she rose, and fell on his breast, sobbing.

Wild and speechless was that last embrace. The moon, which had witnessed their union by the heathen grave, now rose above the tower of the Christian church, and looked wan and cold upon their parting.

Solemn and clear paused the orb—a cloud passed over the disk—and Edith was gone. The cloud rolled away, and again the moon shone forth; and where had knelt the fair form and looked the last look of Edith, stood the motionless image, and gazed the solemn eye, of the dark son of Sweyn. But Harold leant on the breast of Gurth, and saw not who had supplanted the soft and loving Fylgia of his life—saw nought in the universe but the blank of desolation!